KOYASAN

This book has been specially written and
published for World Book Day 2006.

World Book Day is a worldwide celebration of
books and reading, and was marked in over 30
countries around the globe last year.

For further information please see
www.worldbookday.com

World Book Day in the UK and Ireland is
made possible by generous sponsorship from
National Book Tokens, participating
publishers, authors and booksellers.
Booksellers who accept the £1 World Book Day
Token themselves fund the full cost of
redeeming it.

Other titles by Darren Shan

THE DEMONATA

THE SAGA OF DARREN SHAN

DARREN SHAN

KOYASAN

HarperCollins *Children's Books*

SEEK OUT THE SPIRIT OF

DARREN SHAN

ON THE WEB AT

WWW.DARRENSHAN.COM

First published in paperback in Great Britain by
HarperCollins *Children's Books* 2006
Harper Collins *Children's Books* is a division of HarperCollins *Publishers* Ltd
77-85 Fulham Palace Road, Hammersmith, London, W6 8JB

www.harpercollinschildrensbooks.co.uk

Copyright © Darren Shan 2006

ISBN-13: 978 0 00 722138 7
ISBN-10: 0 00 722138 X

Darren Shan asserts the moral right to be identified
as the author of the work.

Printed and bound in Great Britain by
Bookmarque Ltd, Croydon, Surrey

THE BRIDGE

KOYASAN STOOD NERVOUSLY by the narrow stone bridge, chewing a clove of garlic. She was all alone and as miserable as a two-legged crab.

That morning, when she awoke, she had happily said to herself, "This is the day. I will go to the graveyard with the others and cross the bridge." It seemed so easy when she thought about it. Just walk out there, set foot on the bridge and take one small step at a time. Not think about the evil spirits on the other side, lurking beneath the mud-stained tombs or behind the crumbling headstones. Just set her sights on the opposite bank of the stream and cross.

The happiness stayed with her while she munched a couple of dry cakes and fetched water from the well. She smiled as she dressed her younger sister, Maiko, and helped her mother cook breakfast. She laughed as she skipped with Maiko towards the graveyard, imagining how surprised the other children would be when they arrived to find her perched on top of a tomb.

The laughter faded as she passed the two trees which formed the rear gate of the village. Snarling, demonic faces had been carved into the bark of each, and the grooves had been filled with bright red and yellow paint. They had been put there to frighten off any evil spirits who might approach the village during the night. Not the spirits from the graveyard — they couldn't cross the stream. But there were lots of other spirits at large in the world.

Koyasan knew she shouldn't look at the faces. They always scared her. But her eyes wouldn't let her pass without a quick glance left and right. When she saw the fierce, ugly, threatening faces, her stomach tightened and she moved a bit quicker. It was surely her imagination, but she thought the faces had shimmered, that the jaws had widened slightly, that the eyes had narrowed. And the trees themselves had seemed to breathe out.

She walked less confidently after that. Beside her,

Maiko had taken no notice of the trees. But Maiko wasn't scared of much. She was young and didn't know enough about the world to be afraid of it.

But Koyasan still planned to cross the bridge. This was going to be the day. The sun was sizzling, no clouds in the sky. All the spirits would be at rest in the shadows or beneath the earth. As long as she stayed in the open, no harm could befall her.

When she got to the bridge, she found that she wasn't the first to arrive. Some of her friends were already running around the headstones in the graveyard, tumbling over the tombs, chasing each other like playful cats. They shouted hello when they saw Koyasan, but didn't call for her to join them. Every child in the village knew she was terrified of the graveyard's evil spirits. None expected her to ever cross the bridge, and most had given up trying to convince her.

But today she'd prove them wrong! Koyasan believed in her heart that she wasn't a coward. Last year, when a goat had fallen down a steep cliff, and the boys herding it had stood at the top, crying and afraid, Koyasan had climbed down and dragged the goat up. When she fell and cut her arm open once, and the blood flowed like wine, she hadn't cried, not even when Itako stitched the cut closed, pushing a long curved needle in and out of Koyasan's flesh.

There was almost nothing physical that Koyasan was afraid of. But spirits... detached, wretched souls... ghostly creatures of the other world... they were a different matter.

When Maiko saw the trio playing, she gave a gurgle of delight and tottered directly over the bridge to chase after them, even though she was too small, and her legs too stumpy, to catch any of the older, swifter children.

Koyasan dug a clove of garlic out of her skirt pocket and bit into it. She loved garlic and always carried a clove or two around. As she chewed, she stared at the bridge. It was an ordinary stone bridge. It had been built a long time ago and repaired in several places over the decades. A gentle stream gurgled along beneath it. Even in the worst winter, the stream never threatened to overflow. But it never went dry in summer either, although Koyasan often worried that it would, leaving the village unprotected from the spirits who massed and cavorted at night on the other side of the thin trickle of water.

The graveyard beyond the bridge was ancient and sprawling, and no longer in use. People's ashes had been buried there for hundreds, maybe thousands of years. Nobody in the village knew where all the dead had come from. There must have been large towns or a city nearby at one time, but no ruins of such places existed any more. Or else this had been a place of pilgrimage in the past and the ashes of the dead had been brought from far away to rest in this secluded spot.

The land just beyond the bridge was flat and bare – except for the monuments to the dead – but started to rise sharply after seventy or eighty paces. Twenty paces beyond that, the first trees sprouted, and they covered the rest of the hill where the bulk of the dead were buried.

It was impossible to say how many urns of human ash had been set here by their unknown ancestors. There'd been many attempts to find out. One count put the number at ten thousand, another at twenty thousand. One problem was that many of the tombs and headstones had been covered by moss, bushes or trees, and now lay hidden beneath the forest floor, lost forever. Another was that although a headstone might bear only one name, there might be fifty or a hundred urns beneath it, maybe more.

Some said a hundred thousand souls had been

placed here, that the hill was not a natural growth, but had been built out of the remains of the dead. Koyasan didn't think that was true, but she often had nightmares about it, pursued through her dreams by an army of wailing spirits.

Koyasan had never explored the forested, tombstone-encrusted hill. She'd never even crossed the stone bridge which linked the world of the living to the realm of the dead. Fear always stopped her here, on the safe, human side of the stream.

It was silly, she knew. The spirits were wicked, everyone agreed about that. Nobody ever crossed the bridge once the sun had set and most made sure they got out of the graveyard at least an hour before darkness fell, just to be safe. But no spirit could roam freely by day. Some of the stronger ones could maybe exist above ground in the daytime, but they couldn't leave the safety of the shadows. They were forced to cringe behind larger monuments, in the shade of great rocks, or in the hollow stomachs of the thicker trees. As long as you didn't venture too deep into the forest, and stayed out of caves and other dark places, you were perfectly safe. All the children said so. And the fact that they always came back, alive and uninjured at the end of each day, was proof that it was true.

But Koyasan was scared despite all that. She could sense the spirits slithering through the earth like impossibly long, vicious worms, scratching at the surface from beneath, always yearning to escape… capture… torture… kill…

Two claws scraped the back of her neck.

Koyasan screamed, dropped her clove of garlic and whirled round.

Yamadasan was standing there, holding a forked stick, laughing. Mitsuo and Chie were with him. They were laughing too.

"You thought it was a spirit!" Yamadasan chortled.

"Shut up!" Koyasan shouted angrily, automatically bowing — she was always polite, even when scared. "I thought it was a bird."

"No, you didn't. You wouldn't have screamed if it was just a bird."

Yamadasan did a short, mocking dance, then threw the stick away and grinned at Koyasan. "Are you coming across today or staying here as usual?"

Koyasan opened her mouth to tell him she was coming, that today she was going to prove how brave she was… then closed it slowly, not so certain now that she could follow through on her earlier decision.

"Leave her alone," Mitsuo said, smiling softly at Koyasan. "It's not her fault she's scared."

"I'm not scared!" Koyasan snapped, then stubbed the ground with her toes. "I just don't think we should disturb the dead. It's not right to play in a graveyard."

"Nonsense," Yamadasan said. "Nobody cares as long as we don't do any damage. You're just afraid a spirit will jump out of the ground and eat you."

Koyasan glared hatefully at Yamadasan, but there was nothing she could say in her defence.

"Come on," Chie said, patting Yamadasan's back. "We have to go back soon — goats won't herd themselves. Let's not waste time here."

Yamadasan shrugged, laughed one last time at Koyasan, then darted over the bridge, yelling at those on the other side, declaring himself to be a wolf and promising to rip out the guts of the first child he caught. Chie and Mitsuo raced after him, howling gleefully, shredding the silent shroud of the graveyard.

Koyasan stared miserably after the three children, then at the bridge, then down at her feet. She told them to move. A toe twitched, but otherwise her feet ignored her. She looked up at the bridge again, remembering what she'd said that morning.

"I have to do it," she muttered. "They'll make fun of me all my life if I don't."

Summoning all of her courage, Koyasan forced her right foot to rise, then move forward. It hovered in the air a moment, then came down... on the bridge.

A shock of cold air swept through her. The boys and girls in the graveyard were still shouting, howling and cheering, but Koyasan no longer heard them. She couldn't see them either. The world had become a wide grey void. She could hear deep, rasping, breathing sounds, the breath of creatures which had been human once, but weren't any more.

Slowly, painfully, fearfully, she dragged her left leg forward. She had both feet on the bridge now, the first time ever. She stood, suspended above the stream, caught between worlds, petrified at the thought of going forward, desperate not to lose her nerve and go back. She felt sick and her head pounded, the way it had when she'd been struck by fever some years ago.

She realised she wasn't breathing and could feel her face turning red, then blue. The sounds of the dead changed. They were excited now. If she died here, she'd become one of them, and they would have something new to play with and torment. She sensed them reaching out to her, long, misty tendrils which were only vaguely like fingers.

With a scream that shocked the other children and stopped them in their games, Koyasan broke the spell holding her in place. She paused only long enough to suck in a quick, shallow breath. Then she turned and fled, back to the village, leaving Maiko in the care of her friends, sobbing as fear sped her further and further away from the plain, stony, unremarkable bridge.

ITAKO

KOYASAN SPENT THE rest of the day working hard. She helped her mother wash clothes, then fixed a hole in the roof of their house with her father. That wasn't a girl's job, but since he had no son, Koyasan's father often treated his eldest daughter like a boy, letting her work with him, teaching her how to wrestle and whistle.

After that, she went through her clothes, searching for loose buttons or little rips which needed stitching. Koyasan liked to look her best at all times. If she was playing and tore her skirt or stained her shirt, she'd rush home instantly to mend the hole or wash out the stain.

That took her up to lunch. Most of the children ate a quick lunch, then gathered at the old graveyard while the adults sheltered from the harsh noon sun and slept. Koyasan would usually eat quickly too, and go and watch her friends play. She didn't enjoy being cut off from the games by the stream, but by watching, at least she felt like she was part of the fun. And occasionally, some of her friends would play with her on the safer, more boring side of the bridge.

But today Koyasan ate slowly and stayed in the village. She was still shaking from her experience on the bridge that morning and had no wish to go anywhere near it for at least a couple of days.

It was the quietest time of the day, the air heavy with snores. Koyasan tried to sleep but couldn't. So she went walking instead, pretending that the houses were giant tombs and that she was in a graveyard of her own, a secret place, far more exciting than the dull old graveyard across the stream. She fought imaginary spirits, jabbing at them with a stick which passed for a sword, chopping off heads, running them through, laughing as they—

"What are you doing?"

Koyasan gasped and dropped the stick. She hadn't expected anyone to see her at play. Glancing around, she saw Itako sitting on the doorstep of her cottage, regarding Koyasan with a curious but not unfriendly expression. Itako was one of the oldest people in the village. She was a woman of many talents — a teacher, doctor, storyteller, law-maker. There were also rumours that she could see into the future and speak with the dead, but Koyasan wasn't sure if they were true or not.

"I was playing," Koyasan said, bowing and smiling sheepishly.

"You should play more quietly," Itako said. "If I'd been sleeping, you would have disturbed me."

"Sorry."

Itako waved the apology away. "Who were you fighting?" she asked.

"Spirits," said Koyasan.

"With a sword?" Itako tutted. "You won't kill spirits like that. In fact, you can't kill them at all — they're dead already."

"I know." Koyasan lowered her head to hide her shame. "I was only playing."

"You should always deal with spirits correctly, even when playing," Itako said. She patted the space on the step beside her. Koyasan didn't want to sit down, but it would be impolite not to.

"Why aren't you playing with the others?" Itako asked.

Koyasan didn't answer.

"Do they tease you? Bully you? Are you a loner?"

"No."

"Then...?"

"I don't like the graveyard," Koyasan muttered.

"Hurm." Itako studied the girl for a few seconds. "Or maybe it's spirits that bother you more?"

Koyasan nodded quickly.

"They can't come out in the day," Itako said.

"I know. But they scare me anyway. I can still feel them, even if I can't see them."

"Oh?" Itako leant forward for a closer look — her eyes were no longer as sharp as they'd once been. "You're Koyasan, aren't you? I remember when you cut your arm. Let me see the scar."

Koyasan held her arm out. Itako rubbed a finger over the thin line and grunted. "Not bad, even if I do compliment myself." She ran her fingers down to the end of Koyasan's arm and gripped the girl's hand. She tickled Koyasan's palm with her thumb and Koyasan smiled.

"You will need help soon," Itako said softly. Koyasan squinted at her uncertainly. "Don't be afraid to come to me, even if you feel like you can speak to no one. If I have the power, I will do what I can to make your task easier."

"I… I don't understand," Koyasan stuttered. "Am I in trouble?"

"Not yet," Itako said. "But you soon will be."

"What sort of trouble?" Koyasan's heart was fluttering like a bird's and she found it hard to speak.

"I don't know," Itako said and released Koyasan's hand. She waved to show that Koyasan could go.

As Koyasan stood shakily and stepped away, Itako called after her. "Most people feel fear at some time in their life. That doesn't make them cowardly. Cowards are those who do nothing when their fear threatens to destroy them. You must face your fear when you have to. If you do, you might not survive, but if you die, you won't die a coward."

While Koyasan was trying to think of something to say in response to that, Itako rose – slowly, because she was an old, tired woman – and went inside, where it was cooler, to rest from the hot midday sun. She did not say goodbye to Koyasan. She knew they would be meeting again soon.

GRAVY

IT WAS A Holy Day. Nobody in the village worked on a Holy Day except those who had to milk goats or herd sheep, but even they took time off to pray and relax. It was the day when, by tradition, all of the children went to the graveyard to play and chase each other. They had to return at certain times to pray, and for meals, but most of the day was usually spent among the tombs, headstones and trees of the hill. Their parents often came to watch them at play, sitting on the banks of the stream, snacking, meditating or simply relaxing.

Koyasan usually spent a lot of time with her mother and father on Holy Days. They'd sit together on the village side of the bridge. Her parents would chat with other adults, while Koyasan would play with the babies and younger children who were not old enough to play in the graveyard.

Today though, she didn't want to be anywhere near the place. It was only three days since her run-in with Itako and she'd barely slept. She kept thinking of all the terrible things that might happen, preparing herself for the worst. She wasn't sure what that worst might be, but she guessed it would have something to do with the graveyard and the spirits, since Itako had mentioned Koyasan having to face her fears, and the graveyard was what she was most afraid of.

"Wanna go gravy!" Maiko cried, waving her short arms at the bridge. She couldn't say 'graveyard' yet.

Koyasan's mother smiled at Maiko, then at Koyasan. "Do you want to take her to play with the others?" she asked.

Koyasan shook her head wordlessly.

"Still afraid of the spirits?" her father chuckled, giving her a hug. "That's fine. You don't have to go anywhere you don't want to."

Her parents had tried many times to convince her to cross the bridge, but when they finally realised she was genuinely terrified of the graveyard, they stopped trying to force her.

Koyasan eyed the bridge and graveyard with growing unease. She didn't even want to be this close to the home of the dead, regardless of the protective stream.

"Can I go?" she asked her mother.

"Go where?" came the reply.

Koyasan shrugged. "It's too hot," she lied. "I want to play somewhere else. I'll take Maiko." Her parents expected Koyasan to babysit her younger sister on Holy Days. She knew they'd be more likely to let her leave if she took Maiko with her.

"Are you sure?" her mother asked. She put a hand to Koyasan's forehead. "You're not sick?"

"No," Koyasan said. "I want to play with Maiko, but it's too hot here. I might take her to the waterfall."

"Very well. Do you have food?"

"Some garlic."

Koyasan's mother rolled her eyes. "You and your garlic! Here, take some bread for Maiko. I'll cook a few extra dishes for supper — you'll both be hungry after such a long walk."

The waterfall was a two-hour walk away, a bit shorter coming back since most of it was downhill. Koyasan hadn't intended to go there today, but now that the thought had popped into her head, she was delighted. It was the perfect place if you wanted to get away from graveyards and dark feelings.

"Come on," Koyasan said, grabbing one of her sister's pudgy hands.

"No!" Maiko protested. "Wanna go gravy!"

"No gravy today," Koyasan smiled. "Not unless we have some for supper."

Maiko scowled at the weak joke and wrenched her hand away. "Go gravy!" she snorted and raced towards the bridge, knowing Koyasan wouldn't dare come after her if she got to the other side.

Koyasan laughed. Her legs were much longer than Maiko's and she could run a lot faster. She gave her little sister a lengthy head start, enough to let her think that she might make it to the bridge. Then, with a wild cat's shriek, she pursued Maiko and swept down on her like a gust of wind from a mountain.

Maiko squealed with pretend terror as Koyasan whirled her off her feet and carried her away from the bridge. But when she realised she was trapped, and that Koyasan wouldn't set her down again, she began to slap her sister and cry.

"Wanna go gravy!" she wailed.

"No," Koyasan said, hurrying away from the bridge, as much to get out of earshot of her parents as to escape from the graveyard. "We're going to the waterfall. That's much nicer than the graveyard."

"Wanna play!" Maiko shouted.

"You can play. With me. At the waterfall."

"No! In gravy!"

Koyasan ignored her struggling sister's protests and pushed on doggedly. She was soon on the path to the waterfall, walking beneath leafy, shady trees. She felt much better now, the lightest she'd felt in three days. After a while, she set her sister down.

"Hate you!" Maiko roared, kicking Koyasan's shin.

Koyasan sniffed and walked on, sure that Maiko would follow.

"Gravy!" Maiko yelled. "Gravy! Gravy! Gravy!"

Koyasan sensed the younger girl turn and march back towards the village. She smiled to herself and didn't slow or look back. A few moments later she heard Maiko stop. Koyasan began counting inside her head. When she got to six, there was a rush of footsteps and Maiko popped up beside her.

"Gravy," Maiko said miserably, but it was no longer a demand.

"You can go to the gravy next week," Koyasan said.

And they walked on together, through the trees, up the hill to where the waterfall was waiting.

SULKING GIRL

THE WATERFALL WAS nothing spectacular, not much taller than Koyasan. But it fell into a nice deep pool with fish in it, and there were lots of colourful wild flowers growing around the edges.

Several adults were resting by the pool and a couple were swimming. One pair had a baby, even younger than Maiko, but otherwise the two sisters were the only children there.

Maiko's mood improved when she saw the pool. With Koyasan's help, she wriggled out of her clothes and charged into the water, yelling happily. Koyasan undressed and joined Maiko. The fish nipped at her feet and calves, but left her alone once she moved further in and drew her legs up, to float.

Maiko couldn't swim yet, so she stood in the

shallower water near the bank. She roared at the fish as they bit her, and kicked out at them. But the bites didn't really hurt. She was just playing with the fish, pretending to be angry.

The girls spent most of the afternoon at the pool, swimming or sunbathing, making up games. They ate the bread and Koyasan shared a garlic clove with Maiko. As the day wore on, Koyasan thought about returning home, but Maiko kicked up a fuss each time Koyasan tried to lead her away from the pool. She'd been disappointed once already today, and wasn't going to stand for another order from her older, bossy sister.

Koyasan could have dragged Maiko away if she'd wished, but she was enjoying herself. So she let Maiko have her own way, even though she knew their mother would be worried if they returned home late.

Eventually, with the sun dropping in the sky, she had to be firm. If they left now, they'd arrive home a good hour before sunset. But if they left any later, and got delayed on the way, the sun might beat them to it, and Koyasan had no intention of ending up stranded outdoors in the dark.

Most of the adults had left, and the few who remained were not from Koyasan's village, so the girls had to walk home alone. Maiko was tired and grumpy, and threw a tantrum when Koyasan peeled her away from the pool.

"Don't wanna go home!" she shouted.

"We have to," snapped Koyasan. "It will be dark soon."

"Don't care!" Maiko yelled.

Koyasan was tired too, so instead of laughing off Maiko's protests, as she had earlier, she argued with her on the walk back. She lost her temper and called Maiko all sorts of foul names, making her cry. In response, Maiko dragged her feet and tried to run away a few times, almost losing Koyasan at one stage when she darted through a hole in a thick bush that Koyasan couldn't fit through.

Because of the arguing and delays, the walk back took longer than Koyasan had planned, and it was nearly sunset by the time they came to the place by the stream from which they'd set out hours earlier. Everyone had gone back to the village. Koyasan could see lights twinkling through the trees and she could smell lots of wonderful food. She'd been worrying about the time, not sure they'd make it home before dark, but when she saw the lights, she relaxed.

"Gravy," Maiko said, as they drew level with the bridge. She tugged hard on Koyasan's arm and began singing, "Gravy! Gravy! Gravy!"

Koyasan knew Maiko didn't really want to go into the graveyard. It was late, she was tired and there were no other children there for her to play with. She was only doing this to annoy Koyasan.

"Go on then!" Koyasan yelled, losing her temper again. She released Maiko and pushed her away. "Go to the graveyard if you want. I won't stop you."

Maiko blinked up at her older sister. She hadn't expected this and wasn't sure what to do. Koyasan laughed at her hesitancy and began to tease her. "Maiko's afraid of the graveyard! Fraidy rat, fraidy rat, fraid as a rat who can smell a fat cat!"

Maiko's face darkened. "*You* the fraidy!" she snarled, then turned and stomped across the bridge.

Koyasan's smile faded when Maiko reached the far side of the bridge and stepped off. It wasn't night yet, but it was close to it, and the stronger spirits might be able to tolerate weak evening light like this.

"Come back!" Koyasan called. "Let's go home. I'm hungry."

Maiko heard the fear in Koyasan's voice. She grinned and stuck her tongue out. "Come get me!"

"Don't be stupid," Koyasan growled. "Come back quick, before the sun goes all the way down."

"Wanna play," Maiko insisted.

"You can't," Koyasan said. "Everybody's gone home. There's nobody there except you... and the evil spirits."

Maiko's wicked smile disappeared when Koyasan said that. She glanced around nervously, noticing the shadows and eerie emptiness for the first time. The tombs and headstones, which looked crumbling and harmless in the day, now took on a much darker and more threatening appearance. Koyasan saw Maiko make up her mind to return. She took one step forward, back on to the bridge...

...then stopped when someone laughed. It was a child's laugh and it came from within the cover of trees near the base of the hill.

Maiko's face lit up again and she smirked at Koyasan. "Play in gravy!" she crowed.

"No!" Koyasan gasped. "You don't know who that is. It might not even be..."

But Maiko had already spun around and was racing away from the bridge, hurrying towards the spot where the laughter had come from. Koyasan yelled after her, calling her back, but Maiko ignored her and, seconds later, vanished from sight into the forest of trees, where the roots of the giant trunks mixed with the urns and ashes of the dead.

THE WAIT

KOYASAN WAS COLD, and not just because the sun had set. It was twenty or thirty minutes since Maiko had entered the forest which grew above the remains of the ancient dead and there'd been no sign or sound of her since. Koyasan had called her name several times, but there hadn't been an answer, not even an echo — the dead swallowed echoes out here.

The shadows of night were swiftly stretching across the world, claiming the graveyard and the village. The sun had dipped completely out of sight and soon it would be night proper. Koyasan was safe where she stood, protected from the evil graveyard spirits by the stream. But Maiko wasn't. She was in the midst of them, on the hill, maybe lost in the forest. And if the spirits hadn't risen from their slumber and found her yet, they would soon.

"I shouldn't have let her go," Koyasan moaned. "If anything happens to her, it's my fault."

Part of her wanted to cross the bridge and go in search of the missing girl. If there was ever a time to face her fears and overcome them, this was surely it. Go there, find Maiko, bring her back and everything would be fine. They'd be laughing about this later as they ate supper, and Koyasan's mother and father would tell her how proud they were. Yamadasan and the others could never call her a coward again, not after something like that.

But she couldn't move. Her fear was too strong. Maiko was in trouble, she was certain, but there was nothing she could do to help. She couldn't even run back to the village to fetch one of the braver children or an adult to go and find Maiko. All she could do was stand, shiver and stare.

More time passed. Night had taken firm hold of the world, and while the sky was still laced with a few bright streaks, they were dwindling fast. Another five minutes and day would have departed totally.

There were footsteps.

Koyasan held her breath and strained her ears,

praying for a glimpse of Maiko. But then she realised the footsteps were coming from behind her, from the village. Looking backwards, she saw Mitsuo coming with a lantern and a plate of food. She was confused at first. Was he bringing the food for her and Maiko? Then she remembered that it was customary to leave an offering by the banks of the stream on Holy Days. If any hungry evil spirits passed in the night, they would hopefully eat the food and leave the sleeping humans alone.

Mitsuo saw Koyasan's shape and stopped. His eyes hadn't adjusted to the darkness like hers had. He thought this might be an especially hungry spirit, come early to get ahead of the others.

"Wh... wh... what are you?" Mitsuo croaked, taking a step back.

"It's all right," Koyasan said, bowing even though he couldn't see her. "It's me."

"Koyasan?" Mitsuo raised the lantern, waited for his eyes to focus, then edged towards her. "What are you doing out here? Your mother and father are worried. Some of the men are setting out to look for you and Maiko."

"It took us a long time to come back from the waterfall," Koyasan said softly.

"Your mother won't be pleased at you for scaring her," Mitsuo sniffed. "I bet she doesn't let you..." He stopped. "Where's Maiko?"

Koyasan gulped. "She's playing. In the graveyard."

Mitsuo gawped. "The graveyard?"

"Somebody laughed. I think it might have been Yamadasan. She's playing with him."

"Don't be crazy," Mitsuo said. "There's nobody in the graveyard, not at this time. We all left hours ago."

"But there was laughter," Koyasan whispered.

Mitsuo's eyes widened as he realised what this meant. Maiko was alone, in the graveyard, at night, lured in by some nameless creature's laugh.

"I'm going to fetch help!" he shouted. "Wait here. Keep calling for her. I'll give you the lantern."

Mitsuo passed the lantern to Koyasan, made sure she had a firm grip on it – he could see that she was dazed – then ran back the way he'd come, doing what Koyasan should have done as soon as Maiko entered the forest.

Koyasan felt worse than ever. She'd tried to convince herself that nothing was wrong, that Maiko would return unharmed, that there were lots of children in the graveyard, playing a trick on her to scare her. But now she realised just how bad this was. If Maiko had been taken by the spirits because of Koyasan's fear... if her mother and father came and asked where Maiko was and Koyasan had to point at the darkening forest...

She got ready to run. She couldn't face her parents and the other villagers. Couldn't live with the guilt and blame. Better to flee now and never come back. Maybe go to the waterfall and give herself to the fishes, stand beneath the falling water and pray for it to wash her away, to dissolve her into nothingness and...

"Koyasaaaaaaan..."

Koyasan's spine turned to ice. Somebody had called to her from the graveyard. But it hadn't been a human, natural voice. It had sounded like the wind whispering through moss on a headstone or over the exposed teeth of a skull.

With a dry mouth and trembling hands, Koyasan waited for the voice to call to her again. When there was only silence, she shakily stretched forth her lantern, so it was hanging over the stream. For a few seconds she saw nothing except the jutting tombs and headstones of the area beyond the bridge. But then she caught sight of a flicker to her left. Turning the lantern, she readjusted, and saw a shape slide out of the forest and glide down through the tombs towards the bridge.

Something was coming out of the graveyard.

NOT MAIKO

KOYASAN THOUGHT THE thing was a spirit. It didn't move like a human. It seemed to sweep down the hill as if on a sled. Its head never twitched and its arms hung heavily by its sides. Even when the thing swerved to avoid the tombs and headstones, it didn't swivel the way a living creature would.

It wasn't very big, but that meant nothing. Powerful spirits could be the size of a mushroom and still have the strength to turn a man's insides to tar.

Koyasan retreated, backing up slowly, not trusting the water of the stream to keep her safe from this approaching spirit. Thoughts of Maiko and her parents were forgotten. All that mattered now was getting away from this spirit before it surged across the bridge and...

The thing stopped at the opposite end of the bridge. Light from the lantern struck its face. And relief flooded through Koyasan like a tidal wave.

It was Maiko!

Koyasan called out joyously to her sister and hurried to the bridge, beckoning Maiko forward. But Maiko didn't react. She stood on the far side of the stream, separated from Koyasan by the bridge, her face blank, not moving a muscle.

Koyasan's throat tightened. Was this really Maiko? It certainly looked like her, but Maiko had never stood so stiffly. She was always wriggling and smiling, waving her hands or twitching her toes. This looked more like a statue than a living, breathing girl. Koyasan couldn't even see her chest rising or falling.

"Maiko?" Koyasan asked quietly.

No answer.

Then Maiko – if it *was* Maiko – stepped on to the bridge and advanced, taking slow, stiff, sinister steps. Koyasan gripped the handle of the lantern tightly and lowered it, so the light was shining directly at Maiko. Her sister's eyes didn't flicker. Her pupils didn't narrow. She walked on, oblivious, unaware of light or darkness.

Koyasan wanted to run, and she would have, except she could hear people coming behind her. It was too late to flee. Seconds later, her father was lifting her off the ground and laughing, hugging her hard to his chest. Her mother raced past them to grab Maiko. She was smiling.

Koyasan turned her head to watch her mother. She saw her slow before reaching the bridge. A few cautious, hesitant steps... then she stopped. Maiko was still crossing the stream, and their mother had noted the same strangeness in the girl as Koyasan had.

"Maiko?" she called. The tremble in her voice made Koyasan's father squint at his younger daughter with suspicion.

"Maiko?" Koyasan's mother called again as the girl – the *thing* – came to the end of the bridge. She waited there a moment, as though deciding whether or not she could leave the bridge and enter the world of the living.

Then she took the final step, off the bridge, on to the human side of the stream.

Koyasan's mother reached out to the Maiko-shaped thing, but didn't actually touch her. Her hands were shaking. She sunk to her knees and stared into the tiny girl's lifeless eyes. This close, Koyasan could see a sort of mist in the pair of globes, like a thin veil covering Maiko's eyes.

Koyasan's father put her down and went to kneel beside his wife. He called Maiko's name, without response, then laid a hand on her shoulder and shook her gently, fearfully.

Nothing happened.

Behind them, the other villagers were muttering uneasily. They couldn't see what Koyasan and her parents could, but they knew something was wrong. A few started praying aloud, to ward off evil spirits. A burly man — Terani, one of the village elders — stepped forward and told Koyasan's parents to take their daughters home.

"There's something foul in the air," Terani said. "We should not be out here this late. The world belongs to the dead at night."

Koyasan's father glanced at her mother. A silent question passed between them. Koyasan's mother hesitated, then nodded shortly. Together, they picked Maiko up. She didn't move or display any emotion. The pair held her between them, staring at her as if she was some weird animal they'd captured. Then Koyasan's mother wrapped both arms around the girl and marched back to the village, trying hard not to let her fear and uncertainty show.

Koyasan's father watched his wife depart, a troubled look twisting his features. Then he glanced down at his eldest daughter, who was pale-faced and shivering. He gulped, then hugged her quickly and gently prodded her ahead of him. Reluctantly, knowing she was to blame for whatever had happened to Maiko, Koyasan set off after her mother and the Maiko-shaped thing that had taken the place of her little sister.

EMPTY VESSEL

KOYASAN'S PARENTS SPENT an hour trying to provoke a reaction from Maiko. They hoped she might be frozen or in shock, so they wrapped her in warm clothes and sat her next to the fire. They rubbed her flesh hard, slapped her face lightly, pinched and poked her, all to no effect. Maiko remained stony-faced, never moving, staring ahead sightlessly, eyelids never dropping a fraction.

Outside the hut, other villagers mingled, discussing what had happened, fearing the worst. Some were afraid of Maiko. They thought she was one of the dead come to life. If Koyasan listened closely, she could hear them talking about burning or drowning the girl-shaped spirit.

Eventually, Koyasan's mother sat back and wiped

tears from her face. "We must ask Itako to examine her," she said. "She will know what to do."

"Not yet," Koyasan's father protested, fearing the worst and not wanting to admit it. "Let's give her more time. If we wait, she might—"

"No," Koyasan's mother interrupted sharply. "We've waited too long already. I want to know what happened to our daughter and if it's possible to help her."

Koyasan's father sighed, then looked across. "Get Itako," he said roughly, the first indication that he was angry at his eldest daughter.

Koyasan didn't want to leave — she was afraid of the villagers — but she knew better than to argue with her father when he was in a mood like this. Silently she rose and stepped outside.

When the villagers saw her, all talk ceased. They stared at her, expecting an explanation. But Koyasan said nothing, only walked through them — they parted before her as if she was diseased — head held low, meeting nobody's gaze, shuffling towards Itako's hut as fast as she could without actually running.

Itako was waiting for her, sitting by her fire, staring into the flames, a shawl clutched round her throat.

"I've heard the rumours," the old woman said, before Koyasan had a chance to speak. "Tell me what you know. Quick."

The way Itako spoke – like a teacher asking a student to provide her with the answer to a problem – calmed Koyasan. She found herself telling Itako about the trip to and from the waterfall, letting Maiko cross the bridge, the laugh, Maiko running into the forest, waiting, the voice which had called her name, and finally the not-Maiko coming back. She felt like crying when she finished, but didn't want to weep in front of Itako. So, with a great effort, she held the tears back.

Itako said nothing for a while, just stared into the flames. Then, with a grunt that might have been a curse, she stood, picked up several small bags and hobbled out of the hut, signalling for Koyasan to follow.

The oddly matched pair marched through the ranks of villagers. Koyasan kept her head low again, but Itako regarded the crowd with a dark, contemptuous expression. She'd heard the talk of burning and drowning, and it had disgusted her.

In Koyasan's hut, Itako pushed the girl's parents aside and picked Maiko up, displaying no fear. She sat a little bit away from the fire, then examined Maiko closely, whispering to her, chuckling, stroking the girl's hair back from her face, gazing deep into her eyes, opening her mouth to study her tongue. Koyasan and her parents were silent during the examination, awaiting Itako's verdict.

After five minutes, Itako opened one of the bags and poured a small amount of pink powder on to Maiko's tongue. When nothing happened, she opened another bag, mixed a greenish powder into a paste by spitting on it, then rubbed the paste into Maiko's eyes. She waited a few minutes, observing the girl's eyes like an owl watching a mouse hole. When Maiko's eyelids remained as they were, and the mist failed to lift, Itako sighed and cradled the girl's head to her chest.

"She's not a spirit," Itako said. "This is your daughter."

Koyasan and her parents gasped with relief. Fresh tears sprang to their eyes, tears of hope this time. But before they could get too excited, Itako spoke quickly to make them aware of all the facts.

"Her soul has been stolen by spirits in the graveyard. They separated it from her body. This is your daughter's form, but there's nothing inside. She's as empty as a dry well."

There was a long, tense silence.

"What does this mean?" Koyasan's father finally asked.

Itako shrugged. "She will die. Without her soul, she is nothing. She will not eat or drink. You can force her, but it's better if you don't. She will linger for several days, then her body will pass. As for her soul..." Itako shrugged again. "The spirits can keep it alive tonight, but if they don't destroy it by morning, it will dissolve with the rising of the sun."

As Koyasan and her parents stared in shock at the elderly lady and the doomed Maiko, Itako stood and set the young girl down. "There is nothing *we* can do about this," she said softly but sternly, looking from Koyasan's mother to her father. "You must accept it and pray for help. Under no circumstances must you go to the graveyard to try and rescue Maiko's soul." Itako's gaze settled on Koyasan and her cold eyes held Koyasan's in a tight, unbreakable grip. "*We* are helpless in this matter."

Itako stared at Koyasan for maybe another two seconds. Then she looked away and sighed. "I will tell the others what has happened. You should spend this night with your daughter, praying — maybe the spirits will take pity if they hear your prayers. But let

Koyasan come to me if she wishes. Don't stand in her way."

With that, she slipped out. Koyasan's parents immediately rushed to Maiko's side, wailing and clutching at her. But Koyasan didn't move. Instead of sorrow, she was filled with fear. Because when Itako said that "*we* are helpless", there was "nothing *we* can do", Koyasan knew that what the old woman had left out at the end was, "but Koyasan *can*."

THE MISSION

KOYASAN STAYED WITH her parents and Maiko for maybe thirty minutes, trying to convince herself that she'd imagined the hidden message in Itako's gaze and words. All she wanted was to stay by her sister's side and mourn with her mother and father. But she couldn't. Because part of her knew this wasn't over. Her parents and Itako could do nothing to save Maiko — but Itako had hinted that perhaps Koyasan could.

Finally, knowing she couldn't live with herself if she stood by and did nothing when there was a chance to set this terrible situation right, Koyasan told her parents that she was going to see Itako. They only nodded miserably and waved her away, too concerned with the dreadful fate which had befallen their youngest daughter to worry about how it might be affecting their eldest.

The crowd had dispersed around their hut. Everyone had gone home to pray for Maiko and prepare themselves for the hard days to come. Koyasan passed unnoticed by anyone from her hut to Itako's, slipping through the quiet darkness like a spirit of the night.

Itako was waiting for her, sitting by the fire again, but this time studying the smoke patterns above it. "I wasn't sure you would come," she said, without looking at Koyasan. "I knew you understood what I meant, but I thought you might not respond."

"You told me three days ago that something bad was going to happen," Koyasan noted miserably.

"Yes. But I didn't think it would be this bad. And I didn't think the fear would be as strong inside you as it is. Coming here was the hardest thing you have ever done, wasn't it?"

Koyasan nodded, tears trickling down her cheeks, unable to hold them back.

Itako turned. Her face was red from the heat and lined sternly — she had something difficult to say. "If you want to save your sister, you'll have to do much harder things than come to my hut tonight. Your trials have only begun."

"I can save her?" Koyasan cried.

"Possibly," Itako grunted.

"How?"

Itako didn't answer immediately. Instead she scratched her chin and picked at a mole. "I'd go myself if I could," she mumbled. "Or send one of the men. This is a job for an adult, someone who knows much about the world and the workings of spirits. But *you* let Maiko go into the graveyard. *You* were the one the spirits tricked her away from. And *you* were the one they called to. They singled you out when they hissed your name. It can only be you. That's the way it is."

Itako leant forward and crooked a finger at Koyasan. The girl shuffled closer to the old lady. When they were no more than a hand's width away from each other, Itako spoke in a creaky, cautious whisper.

"You have one night and one night only," she said. "In the morning, if it has not been restored to Maiko's body, her soul will dissolve. If that happens, she is damned for certain. But if you can restore her soul before then... return it to its rightful place in her body... all will be well."

"Restore her soul?" Koyasan echoed, frowning through her tears. "I don't understand. How can I do that?"

Itako chuckled softly, without humour. "By crossing the bridge, entering the graveyard and stealing it back from the spirits," she said.

OVER THE BRIDGE

KOYASAN DIDN'T GO home. She knew if she did, her parents would stop her. Bad enough to lose one daughter to the spirits, but if they lost two it would be utterly unbearable. Her parents, like most village folk, were practical. If one child fell down a well, you didn't throw a second child down after her.

A large part of Koyasan wanted to be stopped. It had screamed at her while she'd stood, listening to Itako, absorbing the old woman's instructions and advice. It had roared with every step she took when she left the hut and was roaring still. "Don't be crazy! You'll be killed! Go home!"

Koyasan ignored it. Somehow, finding strength somewhere deep inside her, she blocked out the voice of reason and the cries of fear, and skulked from

Itako's hut to the bridge leading over the stream into the world of the dead.

That was where she stood now, as rigid as Maiko had been when she returned. Koyasan had never been here at night. Never even been outside the village after dark. It was scarier than she'd thought it would be. She'd often had nightmares about this, or had lain in bed, imagining what it would feel like if she came to this haunted graveyard in the dark of night. But this was real. She *was* here. She was going to cross. And the reality was far more terrifying than anything her imagination was capable of making up.

"Three spirits will attack you," Itako had told her, back in the safe warmth of the hut. "One at a time, they will come. You must defeat these three before you can attempt to bring Maiko's soul back."

Koyasan took a deep, slow breath. Her bare feet were cold. Her legs and arms were cold. Her stomach was cold. Only her head felt hot, as her brain sizzled inside its skull like an egg in a frying pan.

There was a half-full moon. She could see the outlines of the tombs and headtones, and behind them the forested hill. Wisps of mist – or the breath of the dead? – lingered around the monuments and trees. No animals moved or made noise, not even owls or crickets. Nothing living ever disturbed the peace of the graveyard at night.

But Koyasan couldn't see any spirits either. That should have given her reason to be hopeful, except Itako had told her it would be like this.

"They expect you to come. When they stole Maiko's soul and called your name, they made a secret pact with you. If you honour that pact, and behave according to the rules which govern the dead as well as the living, they must behave in a certain way.

"The spirits will not show themselves until you've faced three of them individually. If you lose to any of those three, all of the dead can attack you as they please. But if you defeat the three they send against you, they must wait. And, if you act carefully, they cannot come against you at all."

Although Koyasan couldn't see the spirits, she knew they were there, hiding behind the tombs or slithering through the branches of the trees, peering at her, willing her to cross the bridge, drooling at the thought of getting their ghostly hands on a second young girl.

As she stood before the bridge, desperately seeking the courage to advance, Koyasan dug a clove of garlic out of her pocket and raised it to her mouth.

She often nibbled when nervous. It helped calm her. But tonight she stopped, regarded the clove silently, then returned it to her pocket.

"No," she said softly. "That won't help. The longer I wait, the less time I'll have to find Maiko."

"You'll never find her," said the part of Koyasan which thought she was crazy to even try. "Go home. Eat your garlic. Stay away from here."

Koyasan ignored the voice, but it wasn't easy. She rocked forwards and backwards on the balls of her feet, staring into the darkness. She remembered the last time she'd tried to cross, the headache and sickness. If it had been that difficult in the day, how much harder would it be at night?

"Well," Koyasan told herself, trying but failing to chuckle, "there's only one way to find out."

Shutting out the fear, Koyasan walked on to the bridge. She immediately felt a pain in her head, and the bread she'd eaten at the waterfall tried to force its way up her throat.

Gritting her teeth, fighting off both the pain and the acidic remains of the bread, she walked forward quickly, breathing rapidly around her teeth, eyes wide with fear and disbelief. She hadn't truly expected to do this. Up until a few seconds ago, Koyasan thought she'd lose her nerve and run away when it was time to act. She was astonished to find herself actually doing what she'd planned to do. Astonished... and dismayed. She wished now she'd said goodbye to her parents and friends because she doubted she'd ever see them again.

Across the bridge she marched, hands curled into fists, head pounding, stomach quivering, teeth clattering. She didn't feel like she was walking across a bridge. She felt like she was crossing a tightrope. Only it wasn't the drop she feared, but arrival on the other side.

And then, in a rush, she was off the bridge, standing on the drooping blades of grass in the graveyard which she had feared all of her short life.

The pain and sickness disappeared as suddenly as they'd come. For a second, Koyasan was filled with a sense of wonder and achievement. She felt like punching the air and shouting with delight.

But then the first spirit appeared out of nowhere and hurled itself at her, howling with vicious, demonic delight.

THE SNOW BEAST

THE SPIRIT WAS man-shaped, but taller and broader than any man Koyasan had ever seen. It was white-skinned, a shiny, glistening white. It had a blank, roughly etched face, just a hint of eyes, nose and ears. But its mouth was fully formed and larger than it should be, full of long, sharp, icy white teeth — like stalactites.

For a confused second, Koyasan stared at the spirit. It reminded her of something, but she couldn't put her finger on it. Then a memory clicked into place. It didn't snow very often where Koyasan lived, but there had been a heavy fall a few years ago, and Koyasan and the other children had spent a couple of days throwing snowballs at each other and making snowmen. This creature had that same appearance. It was made out of snow.

Koyasan had no time to wonder how a beast made of snow functioned, if it had a heart, lungs, a brain. What she knew for sure was that it had teeth, and if it got its snowy hands on her, it would bite into her with great relish and make short work of her small, fleshy form.

Koyasan could have raced back over the bridge. Escape was still an option. Flee to safety now and her life would be assured. The spirit couldn't cross the stream.

But she had come too far. She was even more terrified than she had been crossing the bridge, but her fear no longer had control over her. She could fight it now, having overcome the obstacle of the bridge. So, instead of retreating, she raced left, into the graveyard, pursued by the hissing snow beast.

She shimmied around headstones and scurried over tombs, the spirit close behind. Her feet were soon scratched and bruised from collisions with hidden chunks of fallen stones and briars that couldn't be seen in the dark. But Koyasan took no notice of such minor injuries. She knew she had a lot worse to fear if the snow spirit caught her.

She had no plan. Survival was the only thought in her mind. If she kept running, the spirit couldn't catch her.

"Unless it doesn't tire," said the cynical voice which had tried to stop her coming here in the first place. "It's not human. It doesn't have muscles. Maybe it can maintain this speed all night. But you can't. You'll tire soon and slow down, and when you do..."

The voice was hoping to dismay Koyasan, to teach her a brutal lesson, to drive home the point that she should have paid attention to it earlier. But it had the opposite effect. Rather than feed Koyasan's fears, the voice let her think about the situation rationally.

"That's right," Koyasan calmly said to herself. "I can't outpace it. If I keep running, it will catch me. I have to face it and try to defeat it."

Now that she was thinking clearly, she recalled what Itako had told her.

"Spirits have no bodies of their own. They're naturally insubstantial. They can only assume a physical body when a human confronts them. They take their shapes from the thoughts of the humans they face. Because we provide them with their bodies, we always have the power to defeat them."

Itako had gripped Koyasan's hands hard, to make sure she understood how important this information was.

"Every spirit can be outwitted because their physical existence depends on the human they're facing. If I went into the graveyard tonight, the spirits I'd encounter would look vastly different to those you will meet. They'd have to build their bodies from the thoughts inside *my* head.

"You can get the better of all the spirits you face because they will be physically dependent on you. Your manners, patterns and weaknesses are theirs. Without you, they are nothing but shadows. Conquering a spirit is the same as overcoming a bad habit, like chewing your nails or spitting. It can be done by studying the problem, thinking about it, then acting to solve it.

"You will panic in the graveyard. That's unavoidable. But you must not surrender to fear. Keep a level head. Think of the spirits who attack as twisted images of yourself. Study them as you would study your reflection in a mirror. Look hard for their weak points. You *do* have the power to destroy or deflect them. You just need to use your brain and have courage."

Koyasan was annoyed that she'd forgotten such key advice. Itako had repeated herself several times, to make sure Koyasan knew how vital this was. But at least she'd remembered before it was too late. Now all she had to do was figure out a way to stop the pursuing spirit behind her.

Koyasan glanced over her shoulder to examine the spirit again. It looked even more fearful than before, its arms spread wide, its mouth seeming to stretch off its face. And had it grown by a head or two?

Wrestling the spirit was out of the question. In a physical fight, it would beat her easily. But then Itako had told her that most spirits could defeat humans in hand-to-hand combat. You had to use your mind to trick them and bring them low.

Koyasan dodged round an especially wide tomb, then studied the spirit for a third time. She noticed a trail of water behind it. The snow beast was dripping as it ran. Although the night air was cool, it wasn't cold enough to sustain snow. The spirit was using magic to keep its snowy body together, but the natural world was threatening to unravel it with nothing more than average, normal warmth.

Suddenly, Koyasan knew what she must do. Coming to a halt, she dug a clove of garlic out of her pocket, bit into it and chewed rapidly, keeping her mouth closed. The snow spirit saw her stop, and grinned. It thought it had her where it wanted her. Slowing, it moved upon her menacingly, growing a bit more, sprouting a fresh row of teeth behind its upper layer.

Koyasan waited, afraid but confident. Her knees knocked together, true, but her feet remained planted where she'd set them. If she was wrong, she'd die. But she couldn't think about that.

When the spirit came within touching distance, blocking out the moon, trees and most of the graveyard, Koyasan leant towards it, as though to cuddle up to its snowy white chest. Opening her mouth less than a nose length's away from the spirit, she breathed out at it.

The hot, garlic-laced breath from her mouth struck the spirit's chest... and it started to melt! The snow beast hissed with surprise and fear, and stumbled away from the small human girl. Its hands clutched at the melting snow of its chest and it tried to fill the holes in, splashing the running water back to where it had come from.

Of course, that only made the situation worse and more snow melted. Now the hole in the thing's chest was the size of Koyasan's head and getting bigger every second.

Calmly, feeling a bit sorry for the spirit, but knowing it would have done far worse to her if it had had the chance, Koyasan breathed out again. And again. Hot bursts of garlic-tinged breath. Each struck the spirit like a hammer. Soon, only a few thin columns of snow were left of its chest. Its head began to slide down, ending up in the spirit's stomach, then melting along with the rest of it.

The spirit managed one last angry hiss. Then it collapsed in on itself completely and fell to the ground as a puddle of dirty water. It splashed out of existence, forcing Koyasan to step sharply sideways to avoid getting wet. And then it was no more, and Koyasan was standing there by herself — victorious!

DRESSED TO KILL

KOYASAN EXPECTED A second spirit to attack immediately, but as she stood, heart now racing with excitement instead of fear, nothing disturbed the shadowy serenity of the graveyard.

Stepping round the puddly remains of the first spirit, Koyasan climbed on to the lid of a tomb and turned slowly, studying the lay of the land. No spirits... and no sign of Maiko's soul either. Itako had told her it would resemble a ball of multicoloured light. But the only ball-like light here was the reflection of the moon in the snow spirit's watery waste.

Koyasan faced the hill of trees and sighed. She'd hoped to fight her battles here, in the open, but hadn't truly expected it. There had never been any real doubt in her mind that the spirits would tempt her into their forest where it was darker, the paths lined with hidden dangers and secret burial places.

Koyasan stepped down off the tomb and started up the hill, breathing as softly as she could. That had been another of Itako's warnings — make no noise. The spirits demanded silence. No screams or happy shouts. Not even a whisper. If Koyasan defeated the three spirits sent to do battle with her and didn't make a sound, the rest of the spirits would leave her alone and she could take Maiko's soul home [assuming she found it]. But if she made a noise at any stage, the other spirits could attack her as a group.

Up the hill she trudged, to the point where the first trees sprouted, like bony hands sticking out of the earth. She paused there, regarding the trees warily. A spirit could be lurking behind any of them, waiting to pounce. Out here, she could see an attack coming. But in there, it might all be over before she knew it had even begun.

"Oh well," she said, but only inside her head. "Maybe it's better to be taken by surprise — no time to worry about it."

Koyasan raised a foot to step forward... then left it hovering in the air.

Something was moving on the floor to her right. A tiny white creature. She guessed it was the next spirit, but was confused by its small shape. Surely a spirit wouldn't operate in so fragile a form. Lowering her foot, she bent and studied the thing on the ground. It was hard to focus because the light didn't penetrate here. But after a while the creature moved into an area where a lone ray of light made it all the way through the branches and leaves, and Koyasan got a good look at it. What she saw brought a rare smile to her face.

It was a mouse. But not a real, living mouse. As Koyasan already knew, no animals of the natural world lived in the graveyard — or, if they did, they kept well-hidden at night. This was a skeletal mouse. No skin, whiskers or guts, only the pale white skeleton of a rodent which might have been dead a month or a hundred years. It moved like a real mouse, even pausing regularly to sniff at the air, although it couldn't actually smell anything.

The spirits must have given life to the skeleton, Koyasan figured, though she didn't know why they'd bother. Perhaps they were bored and wanted a ghostly pet to play with. Whatever the reason, the bony mouse wasn't a threat. Raising her foot again, she stepped over the quivering skeleton and entered the forest.

The temperature instantly seemed to drop by ten degrees. Koyasan shivered and rubbed her hands up and down her arms. She was lucky the snow spirit hadn't attacked her here — maybe it would have been able to survive in the cooler environment.

Up the hill and through the trees she crept, head twitching left and right, glancing over her shoulder every few seconds. Her eyes adjusted to the gloominess after a while and she was able to follow the paths through the trees. But it was a land of mostly impenetrable darkness, fine if you were one of the dead, with no need for eyes, but unsuitable for anyone living.

The desire to call Maiko's name was strong, and Koyasan had to constantly remind herself of the need for silence. Besides, there was no point calling. Maiko's body was sitting by the fire in their hut in the village, her ears and mouth intact on her head. She couldn't have heard Koyasan's cries or replied even if she had.

After an hour, when Koyasan was starting to worry that no more spirits might attack, leaving her to fail when the sun rose, she entered a small clearing and saw a figure sitting on a fallen log, examining its nails in the light of the moon. Her first impression was that this was a living man because the figure was clad in some of the finest clothes she'd ever seen — lush, green, velvet trousers and jacket, sparkling red shoes, and a golden silk shirt inlaid with shiny, oversized buttons, each stitched on with a different coloured thread. The figure was also wearing a long brown hat, ringed by a band of yellow silk, with a feather rising out of the left side of the band.

Then the figure lowered its hand and raised its head, and Koyasan saw that it was no man of this world. Its face seemed to have been carved out of hardened pus and blood, a horrible mess of red, green and yellow. In a strange way the face matched the clothes the creature was wearing, but this only drew more attention to its horrific features.

The spirit had no eyes or mouth, but it knew Koyasan was there because it somehow smiled. Koyasan wasn't sure how she knew the spirit was smiling – it's difficult to smile without a mouth – but it was. There was a low noise, which might have been a chuckle or just the wind rustling the trees. Then the spirit stood and advanced elegantly, walking towards her like an elder marching in a procession, dignified and graceful, its movements in complete contrast to its chaotic mess of a face.

Koyasan backed away. She wanted to turn and run, but not before she'd had a good long look at her foe. She'd learnt from her previous lesson and was eager to get the measure of this spirit, so that she could find its weak spot and defeat it. But whatever this creature was made of, it wasn't snow. The garlic-breath trick wouldn't work a second time.

While Koyasan was backing away and studying the spirit, it picked up a branch and held it out in both hands, letting the light of the moon shine directly upon it. As Koyasan watched, moss grew along the length of the stick. Then it turned black and began to crumble away, rotting at an impossibly fast rate. Seconds later, only a few mouldy shreds of the stick remained, and the spirit coolly brushed these away, stooping to wipe its hands clean on the grassy forest floor.

When it stood again, Koyasan no longer had the sense that it was smiling. The contours of its face now seemed to be trying to crinkle themselves into a vicious sneer. It pointed at her with a long, yellowish finger, and Koyasan knew it was vowing to rot her down to the bone, as it had rotted the stick.

The spirit started towards her, taking longer steps now, picking up speed. It was time to fight or flee. And since she hadn't yet spotted any weakness which she might be able to exploit, Koyasan spun away from the spirit, chose a random path and ran for her life through the forest. The sharply dressed, nightmarishly featured spirit followed in close, fetid pursuit.

A STITCH IN TIME

KOYASAN KNEW SHE had the power to destroy this spirit of decay, but how? She kept thinking about its face and suit, and what it had done to the stick. How could a girl like her defeat a creature as powerful as this? She didn't dare touch it. Perhaps she could lead it into a trap or push it off a cliff — except she had set no traps and there were no cliffs here.

Was the stream the answer? Lead it to the water's edge and shove it in? That might work, but she had no idea how to find her way back to the stream. She'd been lost in the forest after five minutes. She guessed she could keep running and hope to find her way out, but that wasn't much of a plan.

Also, it wasn't using her brain. Itako had been very specific. Koyasan would have the means to defeat all three spirits, but only if she was brave and used her intelligence. Running blindly, hoping for the best, wasn't the answer.

She risked a look over her shoulder. The spirit was lolloping after her, moving as gracefully as before, ducking to avoid low-hanging branches, neatly swerving around the outstretched fingers of thorny bushes. Koyasan was stabbed and sliced all over, but the spirit appeared as immaculate as it had in the clearing.

Looking forward again, Koyasan noticed a large muddy puddle several paces ahead. Not slowing, she leapt over it. Her heels caught the far end of the puddle and she slipped, coming to a crashing halt against a nearby tree.

It took Koyasan a few seconds to regain her feet and she was sure they would be her final seconds. All the spirit had to do was jump over the puddle – easy with its long legs – and it would have her. But, as she shook her head clear and looked up, she saw the spirit pause at the edge of the mud. Its head bobbed downwards, as if it was studying its trousers. Then it edged round the puddle, giving Koyasan the extra time she needed to spring to her feet and flee.

But Koyasan didn't move. She was staring hard at

the spirit, brain whirring. She fixed on its beautiful clean clothes, remembering the way it had ducked and swerved to avoid any snags or stains. She was also thinking of her own fixation with looking neat, and how she would always stop playing and go home if her clothes suffered a rip or stain.

"I created this spirit," she whispered inside her head. "In a way, it's part of me. It acts the same way I do."

The spirit slid round the edge of the muddy puddle and came straight at Koyasan. It gave the impression that it was smiling again. It thought it had her trapped, unaware that it was the other way round — Koyasan was the one pulling the strings.

As the spirit reached for her with its misshapen, miscoloured hands, Koyasan pushed herself forward and snatched at one of the large fancy buttons on the creature's silk shirt. With a quick motion, she ripped the button loose and dropped it. Then she tore off another, and another.

The spirit couldn't scream, since it didn't have a mouth, but nevertheless it made a sort of squealing noise when Koyasan tore off three of its beautiful buttons. Losing all interest in the girl, the spirit bent and picked up the buttons with trembling hands.

It stared at them mournfully, as though they were three of its fingers. Then, not even glancing at Koyasan, it swept away through the forest, heading for whatever nook or cranny it thought of as home, to look for fresh lengths of thread to stitch the buttons back on.

Koyasan watched the spirit depart, grinning broadly. Inside her head, she sang softly, "Two down — one to go! This girl's on a roll!"

PYRAMID

FOR THREE OR four hours Koyasan wound her way through the graveyard forest, following one path after another, looking for spirits and Maiko's soul. But apart from the skeletal mouse, which she caught sight of every now and then, she saw nothing except trees, old headstones and urns.

She was gradually working her way higher up the hill, to the point at the top where none of the children ever went to play, not even the braver and more reckless sorts like Yamadasan. The trees grew at their thickest here, meaning it was always dark. Stronger spirits could roam freely on the hilltop even on the brightest day.

Koyasan was cold and tired, weary of having to force her way through wiry bushes that seemed intent on not letting her pass. She filled with nerves every time she thought about Maiko and the dawn. How much longer was left of the night? Maybe an hour, not much more, possibly less. She'd felt invincible after overcoming the second spirit, eager to face the third and get this over with, certain she'd beat it as easily as the first two. But now she'd started to think she was on a doomed quest. The spirit would never show itself, Maiko's soul would elude her and the sun would rise in a matter of minutes.

"Admit defeat," said the voice inside her head. "You've proved you're not a coward. You can go home proudly. You did your best. Nobody will blame you."

For a moment, Koyasan wavered. She thought about her parents and how they'd welcome her back. Her friends and how amazed they'd be when she told them her story. She'd be a hero, regardless of whether she returned with Maiko's soul or not.

But Koyasan wasn't interested in being a hero or impressing her friends. She had come here for one purpose only — to save her sister. A valiant failure would bring her no comfort whatsoever.

"No," she said silently to the inner voice. "I go back with Maiko's soul or I don't go back at all."

As though the forest had been waiting for her to make such a decision, the branches of the trees ahead of her swayed in a sudden sharp wind, and the bushes gave way. When she pushed through them, she found herself in a domed clearing. It was a large circle, devoid of trees and bushes, but covered high overhead by the leaves and branches of the surrounding trees, which formed a canopy over the clearing, blocking out the sky, stars and moon.

It should have been pitch black in the dome, but Koyasan was actually able to see better than ever. Because at the centre, hovering close above the ground, was a ball of pulsing, glorious light. It was maybe the size and shape of a pumpkin, filled with every sort of colour Koyasan had ever seen and many she hadn't.

It could be nothing other than Maiko's dislocated soul.

Koyasan started forward in great excitement... then stopped. Itako had told her she must face three spirits before she could rescue Maiko's soul. Yet here she was, the soul glowing ahead of her, nothing between Koyasan and her goal. Had Itako been mistaken? Had Koyasan only needed to defeat two of the evil spirits?

It seemed unlikely. Itako had been right about everything else. This wasn't as straightforward as it appeared.

Taking a step back, Koyasan began to circle the dome, preparing herself for an attack. She caught a glimpse of movement close to her right, but it was only the skeletal mouse. It had followed her to the dome and was now mincing along after her. Maybe it thought she had cheese to give it.

As Koyasan smiled at the thought of the mouse trying to eat cheese – the bits trickling through its bones as soon as it gulped a mouthful down – the ground ahead of Maiko's soul trembled and growled. Koyasan thought it was the start of an earthquake. But then the crust of the earth split and something sharp and triangular thrust upwards, and Koyasan knew this was no earth tremor, but the entrance of the third and final spirit.

She watched with amazement as the spirit grew into being. It was massive, far bigger than either of the others. It grew to twice the size of a man... three times... five... only stopping when the top of its head brushed against the roof of the dome.

And what a head it was! The spirit's body was man-shaped, but the head was a huge upside-down pyramid, accounting for maybe two-thirds of its height. It was the colour of clay. It sat on the neck of the spirit, the tip of the pyramid buried in the flesh of the creature's upper torso. Like the colourfully dressed spirit, it had no eyes or mouth. Yet Koyasan was certain it somehow saw her.

The spirit stood in front of Maiko's soul, blocking Koyasan's view. Its arms were crossed over its chest, and Koyasan could sense it secretly grinning at her. She waited for it to move, but it held its position, its massive head steady on its shoulders, as though standing to attention.

Koyasan edged to her left, to see how the spirit would react. It moved when she did, keeping itself between Koyasan and Maiko's soul. Koyasan went faster and the spirit moved more quickly too. She took a step towards it — the spirit did nothing. Another step — no reaction. Another... and she saw the head tilt ever so slightly forward.

Koyasan leapt back quickly and the spirit's head straightened. She understood now how this spirit worked. Unlike the others, it wouldn't chase her. It was content to stand here and block her path to Maiko's soul. If she came too close, it would lean forward and let its head crash down on top of her, squashing her flat.

It appeared that Koyasan had met her match. There was no way a tiny girl like her could defeat a behemoth like this. It didn't have any weak points. If there'd been more time, and she had the proper tools, perhaps she could dig a tunnel and burrow beneath it. But night was drawing on and she had only her hands to dig with.

If she'd met this spirit before facing the others, Koyasan would probably have given up hope and either slunk away, defeated, or tried to dart around it — which would have resulted in the spirit crushing her. But she'd grown as the night progressed and learnt from her experiences with the first two spirits. She knew she could defeat this monster somehow. This thing had taken its shape from her, and because she was imperfect, the spirit must have its imperfections too. It was just a case of putting herself in the spirit's place and thinking about what she would do, and how she could be outfoxed, if she had a head the size of...

Koyasan smiled. It seemed too simple, but she was sure it would work. The thing about spirits was that they *were* simple. No matter how frightening or invincible these creatures looked, they weren't as clever or complicated as humans. They were shades of the dead, mere shadows of the night. And there wasn't a shadow in the world that could stand up against a good strong light.

Koyasan studied the spirit's head, trying to get an accurate measurement. Then she examined the ground, silently counting off paces. She took a step backwards. Another. One more to be absolutely sure. Then, facing the spirit, she smiled politely... and bowed.

Immediately, automatically, bound by the rules of politeness – just as Koyasan was – the spirit bowed in reply.

The neck held its grip on the head for maybe two seconds as the spirit bent, giving Koyasan a scare and making her think she'd misjudged it. But then gravity took control and the giant head came thudding down to earth, snapping the flesh and bones of the spirit's neck and chest, hammering into the ground like a meteor which had fallen from the sky.

A great cloud of dust, pebbles, twigs and leaves rose into the air, filling the dome. Koyasan had to close her eyes and cover her mouth with the top of her shirt, and wait for the dust to settle. When it did, after a couple of minutes, and she opened her eyes, she saw the head imbedded in the earth, the nearest edge no more than a worm's wriggle away from her toes. It had been closer than she'd realised!

She couldn't see the body until she nudged round the head. When she got a clear view of it, she was pleased to see it lying stiffly on the ground, as lifeless as its giant head.

And behind the motionless body, pulsing more brightly than ever, hung Maiko's beautiful soul.

Koyasan felt as if she was erupting with joy as she raced towards the prize at the centre of the dome. She'd won! She had defeated the three spirits, found Maiko's soul and kept her silence. There was nothing the other spirits could do to detain her. They were bound by the rules of their own game. All she had to do was collect the soul, take it home and—

As her left foot came down, the skeletal mouse darted forward, grabbed the side of the foot with its tiny paws and sank its teeth as deeply into the flesh as it could bite. Caught by surprise, Koyasan did two things simultaneously. First, she kicked the bony mouse away. And, at the same time, reacting instinctively, she yelled, "*Ow!*" at the top of her voice.

Before the echoes died away, the dome filled with more spirits than Koyasan could count. They materialised out of thin air with the inhuman speed of bodyless ghosts. And she knew, within the space of a panic-stricken heartbeat, that all was tragically lost.

A SWAP

KOYASAN NEVER GUESSED there would be so many spirits. She should have known, by the amount of tombs and headstones, as well as the legends. But she had never truly believed that the spirits of the dead would haunt the ancient graveyard in such massive, uncountable numbers.

They filled not just the dome, but all the area around it. Koyasan could hear them muttering and cackling beyond the cover of the bushes and trees, trying to push forward to see what would happen next. The dome could only accommodate a small percentage of the spirits. Koyasan guessed that those who were here must be the more powerful and prestigious of the dead... and thus the most dangerous.

Unlike the three spirits she'd faced and defeated individually, these didn't have fixed shapes. They were whirls and bubbles of light, a bit like the ball of Maiko's soul, only larger and duller, shifting and swirling, taking on new shapes as they curled round Koyasan, pressing closer and closer, menace clear in the way they hissed and laughed — not human laughter, but the cold, humourless chuckling of those who'd been tickled by death.

"Sssilly girl," one or more of the spirits said, the words coming from several different directions at once. "Sssso closssse to the prize. Defeated by a humble mousssse."

"I won," Koyasan sobbed, pleading even though she knew it was useless. "I beat the spirits. I found Maiko's soul."

"Yessss," the spirits replied. "But you broke the ssssilenccce. You mussst be quiet around the dead. You mussst ressspect the sssssilenccccccce."

Something icy and jagged scraped the back of Koyasan's neck. She spun away from it, slapping out. But there was nothing there when she looked.

"This isn't fair!" Koyasan shouted, angry tears in her eyes.

"*Fair?*" the spirits snorted with contempt. "What

do the living know about fairnessss? You have a body, flesssh, life. You have other humanssss to play with and the whole world to explore. Ssssso many people to mix with and thingsss to experiencccce. We have nothing, excccept death, each other, thisss graveyard... and your sssisssssster'ssss sssssoul... and now *you*."

The spirits laughed cruelly, and again something scratched Koyasan's neck. This time she didn't react. She was too busy thinking. The spirits were bitter. They sounded angry because they were bored and imprisoned here. Maybe that was something she could use. But how...?

"What will you do with me?" Koyasan asked, playing for time.

"Kill you, of coursssse," the spirits sneered.

"Torture her firsssst," came a voice from somewhere outside the dome.

"Naturally," the closer spirits said.

"We want ssssome of her too," a third voice chimed.

"There will be enough for everyone," the spirits within the dome snapped.

"No, there won't," Koyasan said, seeing her chance.

The spirits went quiet.

"It will be daylight soon," Koyasan pressed on.

"You can't keep me here when the sun rises. You'll have to kill me before that. There won't be time for you to torture me."

"Nonsssensssse," the spirits hissed. "It issss alwayssss dark here. The ssssun can't bother usssss in thissss placccce. We can take all the time we pleassssse."

"I'll fight," Koyasan growled. "You'll have to kill me."

"You can't fight usss," the spirits snarled.

"Maybe ssssshe can," a spirit outside the dome chipped in. "Ssssshe beat the three we ssssent againsssst her. Perhapsssss…"

The spirits began arguing among themselves in muted mumbles. Koyasan stood still, shivering, trying to listen to what they were saying. But their voices were too low. She thought about grabbing Maiko's soul and running, but she'd never make it. At least, if the spirits were talking to her, there was a chance she could convince them to let her go. But if she angered them, they'd fall on her in a furious huddle and rip her to pieces before she could blink.

Finally, the shapes stopped flickering and the arguments ceased.

"You are a clever, courageousssss girl," the spirits said. "You entertained usss tonight. And there'sss no denying you are of more interessst to ussss than your sssisssster."

"Essspecccially asss ssssshe doesssn't have a body," a spirit outside the dome shouted. "If we'd kept her body, like I ssssaid…"

"Sssssilenccce!" the spirits closest to Koyasan roared. When there was no response, they addressed Koyasan again, angrily this time. "We will do a deal. You came here to ssssave your sssissssster. If you agree to our termsss, we will sssend her ssssoul back to her body."

"You'll let her go?" Koyasan gasped.

"Yessss. You have our word and the dead cannot lie."

"What will I have to do in return?" Koyasan asked suspiciously.

The spirits chuckled. "Ssssstay here, of courssssse. With ussss. To be tortured and killed in our own good time."

"No!" Koyasan moaned. "There must be some other way, something else that I can—"

"No," the spirits snapped. "Ssssswap yourssssself for your sssissssster, now, or we kill you both. Choossssssssse!" the spirits crowed, and then everything went silent.

NO

KOYASAN HAD NO real choice. The spirits had her where they wanted her. If she said no to their offer, they'd kill her and let Maiko's soul perish when the sun rose. Koyasan couldn't save herself. The spirits would slaughter her no matter what she did. If she rejected their deal and fought, the best she could hope for was a quick, painless death. But that would mean letting Maiko die too. It would be better if she agreed to their terms and let them torture her. That way, at least Maiko would live. Better one die horribly and one live than both perish.

Koyasan opened her mouth to agree to the spirits' terms … then closed it without saying a word.

There was no need to rush her decision. She had a few minutes to play with. She'd learnt tonight that you should never abandon hope. Her situation had looked bleak each time she'd faced a spirit, and her initial instinct had been to surrender quickly to them. But by delaying and employing her wits, she'd survived.

"Yes," the inner voice remarked drily, "but those were individual spirits. You can't fight or trick this many. You're finished."

"Not necessarily," Koyasan replied silently. "These spirits were human once. You can always bargain with humans. Everybody wants a better deal in life — why should it be any different in death? If I can offer them something more attractive than my torture and murder..."

"Like what?" the voice sneered.

Koyasan didn't respond. She was remembering the bitterness in the spirits' voices when they complained about her being alive, all the people she could mix with, the many things she, as one of the living, could experience. These spirits were confined to the graveyard. Nothing ever happened here. They had nobody to interact with, nothing to break the boredom.

Children came in the daytime, but the spirits could only watch them enviously as they played and enjoyed themselves. And at night they were alone here, nothing new to experience or do, prisoners of eternity. Koyasan could see how hatred had grown and spread here, why they wanted to torture and kill her. They weren't evil by nature — they just wanted to do something different for once, to relieve the misery and boredom.

They thought killing was their only option. Everybody in the village feared and avoided the spirits. There was nothing they could do with Koyasan except murder her, so that was what they'd made up their minds to do. But they were wrong. If Koyasan could conquer her fear, and think of the spirits as lonely souls rather than malicious agents of destruction, maybe they could come to an arrangement by which all of them would benefit.

It was hard to overcome the beliefs of a lifetime. Koyasan had always been terrified of the spirits. She'd been raised to think of them as wholly evil, beyond approach or compromise. But she'd undergone a transformation tonight. The world no longer looked as simple as it had the day before. Maybe the dead were like the living, neither entirely good nor entirely evil by nature, instead moulded by how they'd lived and how other people treated them.

Koyasan gathered her courage, took a deep, steadying breath, then said, very softly, "*No.*"

The spirits didn't have physical eyes, but she nevertheless had the sensation of thousands of eyelids blinking at the exact same time.

"What?" the spirits said, too astonished to make their voices sound ominous and threatening.

"I won't swap."

"But you have to!" the spirits protested. "We'll kill you both if you don't."

"I don't think you'll kill either of us," Koyasan said. "Not when you hear what I have to offer instead of our deaths."

"More deathssss?" the spirits asked eagerly. "Will you go back and trick a lot of otherssss into coming here, to be killed in your placccce?"

"No," Koyasan snorted.

"Then what?" the spirits grumbled.

"If you let us go," Koyasan said, "I'll promise to come back here one night every week… and play with you."

There was a long silence.

"Isss thissss a joke?" the spirits finally asked.

"No."

"You think we want to *play* with you?" They

sounded offended. "We are powerful, wicked ssspiritssss. We are the dead who have been denied the pleasssuresssss of the next world. We exisssst to torment, torture and dessstroy."

"No, you don't," Koyasan said. "You exist because you don't have any other choice. You act wickedly because people don't understand you and treat you like evil monsters. I'm sure some of you were wicked in life, but not all of you. You can't have been. I bet most of you were normal people and it was just bad luck that you ended up stuck here in this graveyard. Right?"

The spirits didn't answer. She could tell her words had troubled them.

"You're lonely and bored," Koyasan said quietly, confidence coming with understanding and sympathy. "You've known each other so long, you probably don't have anything left to talk about. You get glimpses of the world outside, and I'm sure you want to know more about it, how it's changed, what people are like, what's happened to the places you used to live and the people you once knew."

"They're all dead now," the spirits said.

"Yes. But there are records of what they did, stories and legends. But you've no way of finding out any of that because nobody ever comes here to tell you.

"Well, that can change. *I'll* come. One night a week, like I promised. I'll play with you and read to you. I'll tell you all the stories and history that I know, and find out new tales to pass on. I'll sing and dance if you wish, although I'm not very good at that. I'll bring paintings and small statues, and clothes so you can see what people are wearing. If you want to know about sports, I can find out. If you just want to talk, and tell me about your past or your troubles, I'll sit and listen.

"I'll be your friend," Koyasan concluded simply, then waited for the spirits to answer.

HOME

KOYASAN CROSSED THE bridge with Maiko's soul in her arms. It was warm and slippery, and she had to be careful not to drop it. Part of her was still afraid, worried that the spirits might change their minds and attack. But mostly she was calm and carefree. She had nothing to fear in the graveyard at the end of this long, amazing night — and would never have anything to fear there again.

The spirits had agreed to her proposal. There'd been some dissent. A few wanted to rip her to pieces. There were several truly evil spirits, who cared only about hurting and killing. But most were like living people, with the shadows of good hearts. They'd forgotten that for a while and become the monsters they were treated as. But Koyasan had reminded them of their humanity. The majority of noble spirits had quickly put the troublemakers in their place and made them agree to let Koyasan pass safely.

She hurried from the bridge to the village. The sky was brightening above her, ahead of the sun's stately entrance. She could see smoke rising over the roof of her hut. Her parents hadn't slept during the night, keeping vigil by Maiko's side.

As Koyasan passed through the gate, someone moved in the shadows to her left. Glancing around, Koyasan saw Itako standing there. The old woman was smiling. "You did well," she said softly, then returned to her hut. She was too old to waste a lot of time on unnecessary words of praise.

Koyasan's mother and father were sitting by Maiko's stiff, emotionless body. Their heads were bowed and they didn't look up when Koyasan entered and crossed the room. Koyasan said nothing, only held out the ball of light which was Maiko's soul and gently pressed it into her sister's chest. For a moment Maiko's flesh resisted, but then the soul slipped through the tiny pores in Maiko's skin and disappeared into the body from which it had been taken.

A shimmer ran through Maiko. Her legs and arms jerked. Her nose and lips twitched. Then her eyelids flickered. "Tired," she yawned. Her mother and father cried out with shock when they heard that and their heads shot up. They stared at their youngest daughter, then up at Koyasan, who was wilting on her feet, the trials and exhaustions of the night catching up with her now that it was all over.

"Funny head," Maiko said, steepling her fingers together into a pyramid shape.

"Yes," Koyasan agreed.

Maiko reached up and hugged her older sister, then lay down and went to sleep on the floor. Koyasan thought about going to bed, but decided it was too far to walk, so she lay down, cuddled up to Maiko and fell asleep too.

On chairs beside them, their parents watched the sisters sleeping, and slowly their stunned expressions were replaced by smiles of relief, love and joy.

DEAD HAPPY

A LOT OF the villagers didn't believe Koyasan's story. They thought the sisters had played a trick on them, that Maiko had been faking. After all, everybody *knew* that the spirits in the graveyard were evil and would kill anyone who went there at night. This was a truth which had been passed down through generations. Were all the adults, and their parents and grandparents before them, wrong and this young snip of a girl right? Impossible! She was lying. She had to be.

Koyasan didn't care what people thought. She just tried to get on with life as normal. She'd talk about that night on the hill if pressed, but was happier not to. She didn't think it was polite to gossip about the dead behind their backs.

When, four nights later, she returned to the graveyard, a huge crowd had gathered. Most were convinced that she wouldn't enter the graveyard or wouldn't return if she did. Yamadasan was there, ready to laugh at her when she fled from the bridge as she always did. Only her parents truly believed she'd cross, and although they were worried, they'd seen a new strength in their eldest daughter's eyes and knew they couldn't stand in her way. Koyasan had earned the right to make her own decisions.

Maiko wanted to go with her, to play with the funny spirits in the *gravy*. "Not this time," Koyasan told her gently but firmly. "I'll take you another night."

There were gasps galore as Koyasan crossed the bridge, and cries of outright terror when she walked into the forest and vanished from sight. Koyasan only giggled at the villagers' reactions, then made her way to the top of the hill, where the spirits – her new friends – were waiting.

That first meeting was a bit awkward, the way encounters often are when strangers are getting to know each other. The spirits and Koyasan were overly polite, keeping conversation to matters such as livestock and the weather.

That changed over the coming weeks and months. As they came to know each other, they relaxed and opened up. Soon they were talking about all manner of things, laughing and joking, playing games and sharing secrets. Quite a few of the spirits had been children when they died, and some of these became the best friends Koyasan ever had. Others, it turned out, were distant ancestors of hers and they rejoiced when they discovered their shared bloodlines.

For the first couple of months, only Koyasan went into the graveyard at night. The other villagers were wary of her, believing her to be some kind of holy person, with a great spiritual gift. Koyasan could have let them go on believing that, and acted like a lady of mysterious power, but she wasn't interested in becoming a living icon. She kept telling people that she was an ordinary girl and the spirits were normal people — only dead.

Eventually, driven by curiosity, a few of the other children snuck into the graveyard after Koyasan one night, unknown to their parents. The spirits were delighted and made the new visitors welcome, treating them to a spectacular light display, and telling them gory, grisly stories from the past, which the children happily lapped up.

Over time, more of the children, cautiously followed by adults, ventured into the graveyard, and soon the visits became just another part of their lives. They took it in turns to go and keep the spirits amused, bring them up to date with recent political events, teach them the rules of new and complicated games. They sang to the spirits and told them stories, and in return the spirits taught them old songs and tales which had been forgotten by the living over the centuries.

Once a month they held a lavish festival, to celebrate the reunion of the living and the dead. They quickly became the most anticipated festivals of the year. Everyone dressed up in their finest clothes and costumes, and the spirits would twist themselves into the most fanciful shapes they could conjure up. The whole village would spend the night drinking, feasting, singing and parading through the graveyard, only returning to their homes at dawn.

And not only the villagers. As word spread, people came from provinces and countries far, far away to honour and chat with their dead ancestors, to learn the secrets of a time they had never known, and to unwind and have fun — nobody could ever accuse the dead of not knowing how to party!

And so the years passed. Koyasan and Maiko grew into beautiful, strong women. Since she was the eldest, Koyasan was the first to marry and have a child, a sweet little girl called Tomoko. On the night she was born, Koyasan took her into the graveyard to show to the spirits — they loved the fresh innocence of newborn babies.

Although the spirits welcomed all of their visitors, and forged close links with many of them, they shared a special bond with Koyasan. They never forgot that she had been the one to bring the living and dead back together, and her visits were looked forward to more than any other's.

When, after many long and happy years, Koyasan felt the fires of her soul burning down, she asked to spend one last night in the graveyard, alone with the spirits. Nobody objected and all other visits to the graveyard were postponed.

Tomoko — now a grown woman with children of her own — carried her mother into the graveyard and up the hill. She left her in the domed clearing, and although she wept a bit when she said goodbye, she wasn't overly upset. Very few of the living feared dying any more. They knew that if their souls didn't pass on to somewhere better, they could stay here, among their bodyless friends and close to their living relatives, where they need never feel alone or abandoned.

Koyasan smiled as the sun set and the spirits came out. "Hello, old friends," she murmured. "I've come for one last night."

"It'ssss about time you got rid of that old sssshell of a body," the spirits laughed, circling round her, pressing up close to keep her warm.

"Do you think my soul will pass on in the morning or will it remain here?" Koyasan asked.

"Doessss it matter?" the spirits replied.

Koyasan laughed. "No, not really."

Rising with difficulty, she danced round the dome with the spirits, a stiff, slow dance to begin with. But after a few circuits, she felt a weight lift, and suddenly she was dancing freely and gracefully, making the most delightful and intricate moves of her life.

"There," the spirits chuckled. "You never knew you could dancccce sssso well, did you?"

"No," Koyasan said, pirouetting high above the ground. "Can all the dead danccce like thisss?"

"If they wissssh," the spirits said. "There are no obsssstacles when you're dead. You can do almosssst anything you want."

"I think I'm going to enjoy death," Koyasan grinned, sweeping away from her abandoned body, gliding through the trees and down the hill.

She spent the rest of the night dancing around the tombs and headstones of the ancient, joyous graveyard with her ghostly friends, relishing death as she had loved life, realising now that they were, in reality, one and the same. She never once worried or thought about what would happen in the morning. After all, only a fool frets about the light of the dawn when there are all the glorious shadows of the night to experience and cherish.

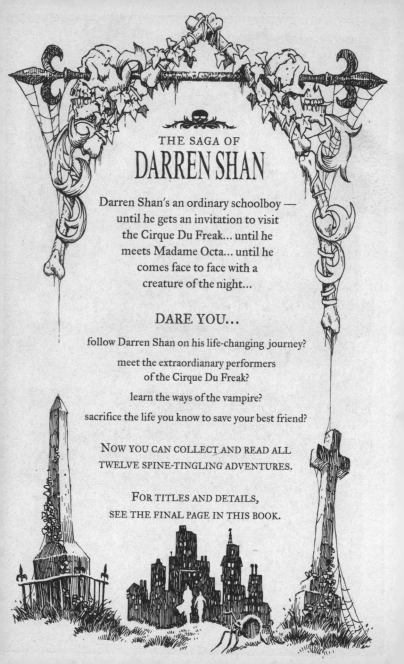

THE SAGA OF
DARREN SHAN

Darren Shan's an ordinary schoolboy —
until he gets an invitation to visit
the Cirque Du Freak... until he
meets Madame Octa... until he
comes face to face with a
creature of the night...

DARE YOU...

follow Darren Shan on his life-changing journey?

meet the extraordianary performers
of the Cirque Du Freak?

learn the ways of the vampire?

sacrifice the life you know to save your best friend?

NOW YOU CAN COLLECT AND READ ALL
TWELVE SPINE-TINGLING ADVENTURES.

FOR TITLES AND DETAILS,
SEE THE FINAL PAGE IN THIS BOOK.